PLANTS
and how they grow

by F. E. NEWING, B.Sc.
and RICHARD BOWOOD

with illustrations by
RONALD LAMPITT

Publishers: Wills & Hepworth Ltd., Loughborough
First published 1965   ©   *Printed in England*

WHAT IS A PLANT?

A plant is any member of the vegetable kingdom. Everything which grows in the ground is a plant: flowers and vegetables; grass and ferns, bushes and trees. In this book we shall find out something about plants and the wonder of growth; how they grow, feed, live and reproduce themselves.

The picture shows a simple flower, the Scarlet Pimpernel, and the basic parts which every plant has in one form or another.

The roots grow into the soil to take in the food which the plant needs, and they also anchor the plant. The nourishment rises through the stem to the plant. The leaves give off excess moisture and absorb the light essential to growth. The flower develops into the fruit and seed for growing into new plants.

There is an enormous number of different kinds of plants, and often a great variety of each kind. Each kind of flower has its own shape, colour and, sometimes, its own scent. But every plant has the basic features shown in the picture—root, stem, leaves, flower and seeds. The more you find out about plants the more you find to make you wonder.

On some pages there are experiments which will help you to understand a little about botany, as the study of plants is called. Other pages describe how plants live, or special kinds of plants. Whenever you can, find examples for yourself and make a note of them.

4

7214 0122 8

COROLLA

CALYX AND
PISTIL

CAPSULE
AND SEEDS

ROOTS

Dig up a Groundsel or a Buttercup, taking care to obtain the roots complete. Shake off the soil, wash the roots under a tap and let them dry.

You will see that the roots have many fibres, all the same length and thickness, so they are called *fibrous roots*. The fibres spread out in the soil and give the plant a strong grip. They also absorb the food the plant requires in the form of moisture. If you look at the root closely you will see tiny hairs on the fibres, through which the plant is fed.

An experiment will show you that roots take up moisture. Put your plant in a bottle of water, sealing it in with plasticine, and mark the level of the water with a piece of sticky paper. Put the bottle on a light window-sill and leave it. In a day or so you will notice that the level of the water has gone down. The roots have absorbed some of the water and have passed it up the plant.

Now dig up a Dandelion with its roots. Instead of a cluster of *fibrous roots* it has one thick root, tapering to a point, with small fibres growing from it. This is a *tap-root*. Tap-roots do something else as well as supporting the plant and absorbing its nourishment from the soil, they store food for the plant to use in the following winter. Carrots and Parsnips, for example, have tap-roots, and when we eat them we are eating the food the plants stored for themselves.

Water level
marked

GROUNDSEL PLANT
showing fibrous root

DANDELION
PLANT
showing tap-root

Small hairs
on roots

STEMS

You can use a stick of Celery to show that the stem of a plant takes food up from the roots. Stand it in a jar of water coloured with a teaspoonful of red ink. In an hour or so you will see thin red lines up the stem of celery, and soon the leaves will be tinged with red. If you slice the stem you will see red dots, which are the tubes through which the coloured water has passed up the stem.

There are many different kinds of stem, as you can see by looking at different plants. Tree trunks are the stems of the trees, and in the same way they carry the food, absorbed in the moisture in the soil, up to the branches for the leaves and fruit.

All stems do not stand up from the ground. Some lie on the ground, like the Strawberry; others climb, as does the Runner Bean, which winds itself round bean-poles. Others have tendrils to cling to twigs as they climb, others have suckers; these are mentioned on page 36.

A Potato is itself a portion of a stem, which remains underground and swells to contain food for the plant. Stems like this are called *tubers*. Yet another kind of stem thickens where it joins the root to form a *corm*, which is also a food-store for the plant. The Crocus is a plant which develops corms.

CELERY COLOURED
BY RED INK

SLICED STEM
OF CELERY

STEM OF
SIMPLE FLOWER

ROCUS CORM

POTATO
TUBER

BUDS

Plants produce two kinds of buds, leaf-buds and flower-buds. If you examine a twig from a tree or bush in the winter you will see the leaf-buds; there is one at the end called the *terminal* bud and others down the twig called *axial* buds.

Leaf-buds contain the future leaves, intricately folded together, and they also produce new stems. Pick a twig of Horse Chestnut, which is, of course, the 'conker' tree, or a twig of Lime, Beech or Sycamore. Put the twig in a jar of water in a light window. As the buds grow you can observe what happens.

First the brown scales will be pushed off by the growing bud and then the pale green leaves will unfold. A new length of stem will grow, and eventually you will have a new twig with brand new leaves. This is the miracle which occurs in trees and hedgerows every springtime.

Flower-buds contain the future flowers, but they do not grow new stems. The flower-buds are protected by *sepals*, which are simple leaves; a whorl or set of sepals is a *calyx*. In the picture you can see the sepals of a flower-bud being pushed open by the petals of the growing flower. Sometimes the calyx opens out, sometimes it falls off. Sometimes the sepals look like a flower themselves. In the Columbine and Larkspur the 'petals' are really coloured sepals.

If you unpick a good plump leaf-bud or flower-bud very carefully you can see how wonderfully it is 'packed'.

LEAF BUD OF HORSE-CHESTNUT
showing stages of opening

1

2

3

4

DOG ROSE
ning flower bud
complete flower

LEAVES

A plant breathes through its leaves, and it also uses them to absorb goodness from the sunlight. The green colour of most plants is due to *chlorophyll*, a chemical in the plant which enables it to make food in its leaves through the action of sunlight. If a mat is left on a lawn for a while the grass under it becomes pale, and dies—because it is not receiving the sunlight.

Leaves also give off excess moisture, as you can show. Put your Groundsel plant in a bottle of water and put a dry plastic bag round the leaves, tying it tightly round the neck. Quite soon you will see beads of moisture forming inside the plastic bag. This moisture has been given off by the leaves.

Examine a leaf carefully, an Elm leaf is a good example. Down the centre is the *midrib*, which is the continuation of the stem. Veins branch off from the midrib, with lesser veins branching from them to form an intricate network which feeds the whole leaf with the nourishment brought up the stem from the roots. This kind of leaf, with a network of veins, is called *reticulated*.

A blade of grass is another kind of leaf; it is the leaf of the grass plant. It does not have a midrib, but a number of parallel veins instead. (See page 40.) Some plants, such as the Daffodil, store their food in special leaves which are tightly packed together in the form of *bulbs*.

One way of recognising a particular plant or a tree is by its leaves. It is interesting to collect leaves. Press them and stick them in a book with their names.

MIDRIB

VEINS

ELM LEAF

OAK LEAF

GROUNDSEL PLANT IN BOTTLE COVERED WITH POLYTHENE BAG

TULIP LEAF

FLOWERS

A flower is the part of a plant which is often coloured and sometimes scented. As well as being beautiful a flower has a practical purpose in the life of a plant, for it produces the fruit and seed from which new plants grow.

Examine a flower carefully, a Buttercup is a good example. Under the petals is the calyx, consisting of the sepals which protected the bud. The petals, delicate in form and beautifully coloured, are the most conspicuous part. Inside you will see the *stamens* and the *pistil*, by which the plant produces its new seeds.

The stamens are stalks which have anthers on top; these are *pollen* bags, or boxes. Pollen is a very fine powder or dust. At the base of the pistil is the *ovary*, or seed-box, in which the flower's seeds are formed.

Insects are attracted to a flower by its colour, by its scent and by the *nectar* stored at the base of the petals. You have seen a bee busy among the flowers, taking the nectar. As it does this it picks up a little of the pollen on the hairs on its body. As it flies about from one flower to another it rubs some of the pollen it has picked up from one flower on to the pistil of another, and then seeds begin to form in the ovary. In due course these seeds grow and, when they are ripe, if they fall on suitable ground they will become new plants.

There is an immense variety of flowers, of many different shapes, sizes and colours, but they all have the same essential parts in one form or another.

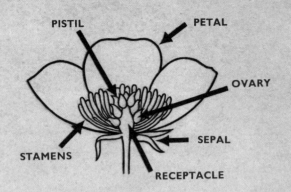

PISTIL   PETAL

OVARY

STAMENS

SEPAL

RECEPTACLE

VARIETIES OF FLOWERS

There are too many kinds of flowers to describe them all in this book, but a few can be mentioned.

The Bluebell and Harebell are, as their names imply, bell-shaped flowers which hang their heads downwards. The flowers of the Convolvulus are more like cones, and the long stems always try to wind round something else. The flowers of the Snapdragon are constructed quite differently, but with all the essential parts. You can imagine they look like little faces.

We all know the Dandelion, the bold, golden flower with many 'petals' and leaves. The Dandelion and the Daisy are called *compound* flowers, because they are composed of many tiny flowers, called 'florets'. If you pull out a single 'petal' from a Dandelion or a Daisy and examine it carefully, preferably with a magnifying glass, you will see that what seems to be a single petal is really a complete little flower itself.

The Pea, and similar plants, have butterfly-like flowers. They are arranged with one large petal, two others like wings, and two smaller ones called the 'keel'. The flowers of Broom, Bean and Gorse are like this.

When flowers are cultivated, that is specially grown, you find many different kinds and colours; as with Roses and Sweet Peas.

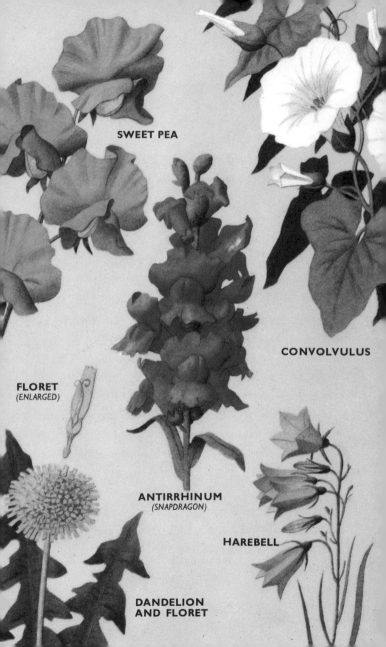

SWEET PEA

CONVOLVULUS

FLORET
(ENLARGED)

ANTIRRHINUM
(SNAPDRAGON)

HAREBELL

DANDELION
AND FLORET

FRUIT

We read on page 14 that when a bee or other insect brings pollen from one flower to another, that is, when it *pollinates* a flower, seeds begin to form in the flower's ovary. Gradually the ovary grows, the petals fall off the flower, and the fruit is left to grow and ripen. Every plant has its own kind of fruit—the fruit of the Wild Rose, for example, is the rose hip, and there are apples, pears, strawberries, pea-pods, acorns, chestnuts and so on.

The fruit contains the seeds which can grow into a new plant—if they fall on, or are planted in, suitable ground. The seeds are inside some fruits, and on the outside of others.

Apple and Pear seeds are the pips in the core. A Gooseberry has the seeds in a juicy pulp enclosed in a skin, and so does the Tomato. Some berries have the seeds on the outside, like the Strawberry. Raspberry seeds grow together in a bunch, each in its own section of fruit. Sometimes there is one single seed, such as the stone in a plum or cherry, where the seed is inside the stone. Nuts usually have a single seed inside the thick hard skin.

Plants usually produce seeds in immense numbers, which is nature's way of making sure the plant will continue. It has been estimated that one Poppy-head, about the size of a boiled sweet, contains about forty-thousand seeds.

ROSE-HIP

APPLE

STRAWBERRY

HAZEL NUT

EA POD

GOOSEBERRY

ACORN

POPPY-HEAD

SEEDS

However small a seed may be, it contains everything necessary to grow into the complete plant, whether it is a tiny Lettuce seed, or a 'conker' which can grow into a great Chestnut tree. A seed contains the plant in its earliest form, called the *embryo*, which consists of two parts. The upper is the *plumule*, the lower the *radicle*. As they grow, the plumule becomes the stem, and the radicle becomes the root. To these are attached either one or two *cotyledons*, or 'seed leaves', which provide the young plant with food until its own roots and leaves have grown enough for it to be independent; then the cotyledons wither away. If you split open a Broad Bean you can see the plumule and radicle of the embryo, and the fleshy cotyledons.

Seeds remain asleep, or dormant, until the conditions are right for growth, as when they are planted in suitable soil. Then they *germinate*, the embryo starts to grow and the plant comes into being.

All seeds do not germinate directly they are planted in suitable soil. Seeds with a hard shell may live for a year in the ground until the shell rots away, and then they germinate. Other seeds, such as Cress, germinate quickly.

Put a piece of flannel in a saucer and damp it thoroughly. Sprinkle some Cress seeds on it and put the saucer in a warm dark place, damping the flannel slightly from time to time. Very soon the seeds will germinate and you can watch the plants grow.

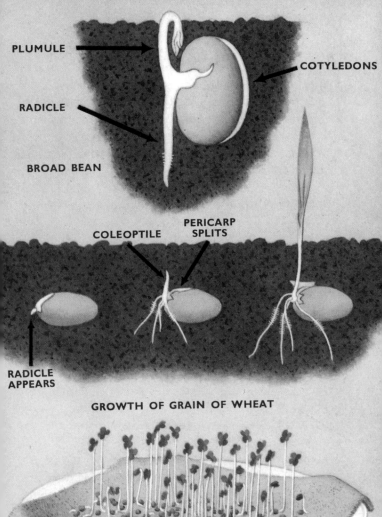

PLUMULE

COTYLEDONS

RADICLE

BROAD BEAN

COLEOPTILE

PERICARP SPLITS

RADICLE APPEARS

GROWTH OF GRAIN OF WHEAT

MUSTARD SEEDS GERMINATING

HOW SEEDS GROW

Four conditions are necessary for a seed to germinate. The first is *moisture;* there must be enough moisture to enable the young plant to burst its hard protective shell. The second is *warmth;* a seed will not germinate unless it is at the correct temperature. The third condition is *air;* seeds must have air to grow. Finally they need *darkness;* they germinate quicker when they are excluded from the light.

Whichever way a seed lies in the soil the shoot will make its way upwards and the root downwards. You can show this by using Beans. Line a jar with blotting-paper and fill the middle with fine soil. Push three beans carefully between the side of the jar and the blotting-paper, each set a different way. Dampen the soil and put the jar in a warm, dark place. Take it out day by day to see what is happening. The shoot will turn upwards and the root downwards.

Plant a dozen or more Beans in a corner of the garden, or in a box filled with earth, and mark the position of each with a little stick. Every few days dig up one of the beans and examine it, studying the growth of the shoot, the roots and the cotyledons. This way you can study the whole process of growth, from the first germination to the final form of the plant. Notice how the white shoot turns green when it comes into the light, how the roots develop and how the cotyledons eventually wither away, as the food store is used up by the growing plant.

THREE STAGES IN THE GROWTH OF RUNNER BEANS

ROOTS AND SHOOTS OF RUNNER BEANS
FINDING THEIR DIRECTION

HOW SEEDS ARE SPREAD

Nature has devised many ways of broadcasting fruit so that seeds are spread, often quite far from the parent plant. Fruit such as apples and plums may be eaten by animals so that the seed is dropped in a new place. The Wild Clematis, or 'Old Man's Beard', equips its fruit with 'feathers' and they are so light that they are taken away by the wind.

Dandelion seeds each have a tiny parachute to be taken by the wind. Some people call Dandelion heads 'clocks', and say that you can tell the time by counting the number of puffs needed to blow them all away.

The fruits of the Sycamore, Ash and Lime trees have little wings, so that when they fall the wings spin and waft the fruit to new ground.

The burrs which stick to the coats of animals, or to our clothes, are fruits covered with little hooks so that animals or people carry them away to fall elsewhere.

Some members of the Pea family use a kind of explosion to spread the seeds. They are bedded in pods, which dry when they ripen until, in the heat of the summer sun, they suddenly split open to scatter the seeds. On a hot day in high summer you can actually hear the pops as the pods burst open and scatter the seeds.

How many different methods of spreading seeds can you think of? And imagine what would happen if all seeds and fruit just fell straight down to the ground; what would happen to the parent plant?

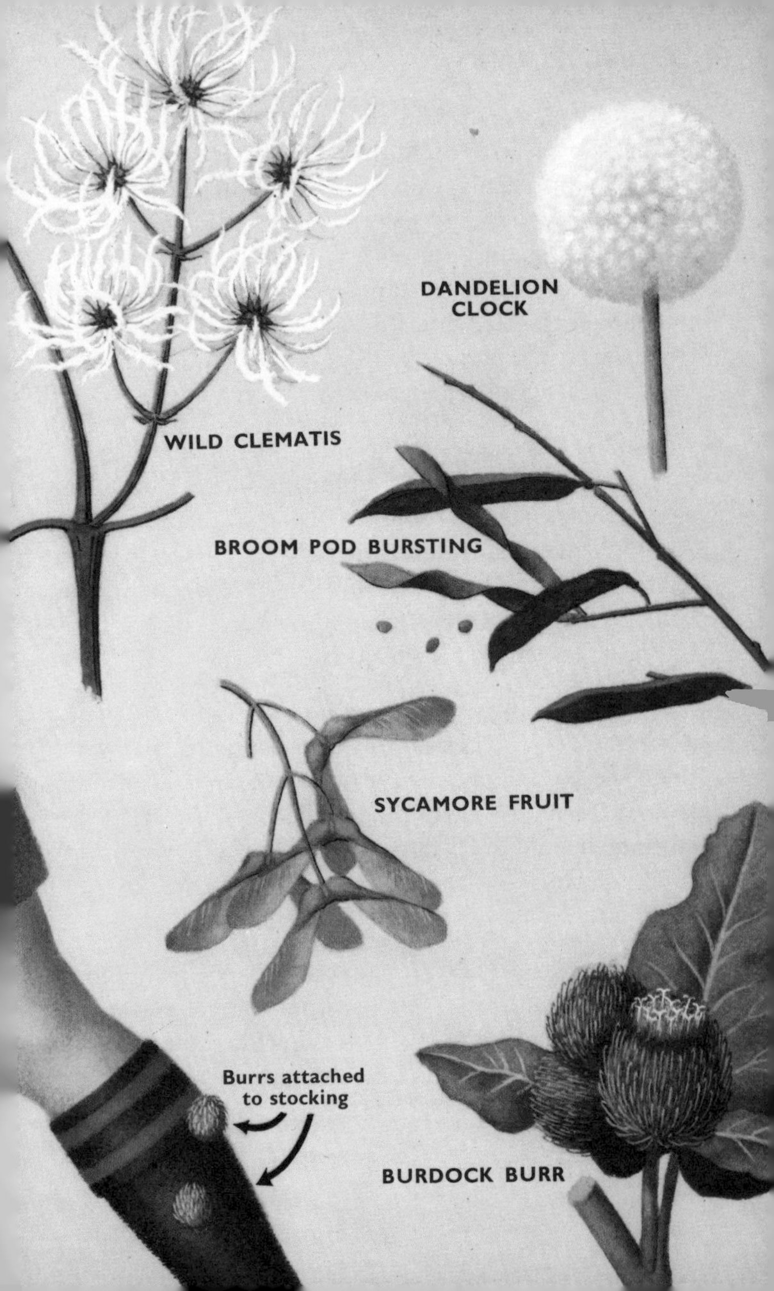

DANDELION CLOCK

WILD CLEMATIS

BROOM POD BURSTING

SYCAMORE FRUIT

Burrs attached
to stocking

BURDOCK BURR

YOUNG PLANTS

Not all plants depend on their seeds to make new plants. Some, like the Strawberry and Buttercup, send out long thin stems, called *runners*, along the ground. After the runner has grown some distance a young plant develops on it, its weight presses the stem to the ground and when the young plant touches the soil it puts down roots. Until it is established it is nourished from the parent plant along the runner, but when it can look after itself the runner withers away.

Jasmine, Bramble bushes and their relations are 'tip-rooting'. If the tip of a branch touches the ground it sometimes makes roots and so starts a new plant. Another method, found with Plum trees and Rose bushes, is for the stem underground to send out 'suckers'. When the sucker reaches the light it turns into a new stem and forms a new plant.

An artificial way of making a new plant is by taking a 'cutting'. You can do this with many plants, among them the Geranium. Cut a tip about four inches long from a Geranium, strip the lower leaves, and plant the cutting in light soil, that is ordinary soil mixed with sand. If you keep the soil moist it will take root and grow into a new Geranium.

Willow, Rose or Privet twigs, about nine inches long, make good cuttings. Put them in a jar of water in a window and watch the roots form. When the roots are well developed you can plant the cuttings out in a good light soil.

SUCKERS FROM PLUM TREE ROOTS

STRAWBERRY RUNNER ROOTING

BRAMBLE TIP-ROOTING

SE CUTTING ITH ROOTS FORMING

GERANIUM CUTTINGS

FOOD, WARMTH AND LIGHT

The food a plant needs is found in the soil in the form of chemicals, and the roots take it up dissolved in moisture. That is why plants need rain, to provide the moisture in the soil.

As well as the correct food, plants must have warmth and light. We sow seeds in the spring when the long warm days of summer lie ahead. You can show the importance of warmth and light to growing plants by two experiments.

Plant Broad Beans in three pots and when the shoots have come up put one on a sunny window-sill, another in the shade, and the third in the coldest place you can find, in a refrigerator if possible. Keep the soil moist and watch. The bean in the sun will grow slowly but sturdily, with good healthy green leaves. The plant in the shade will grow a tall stem, as it seeks to reach the light, and the leaves may be small. The plant in the cold will grow very little, if at all.

Now put a sprouting Potato in one end of a cardboard box and cut a good-sized hole in the other end. Fix two pieces of cardboard to form baffles, as in the picture. Put the lid on and stand the box in the window with the hole towards the light. From time to time take off the lid and see how the potato shoot grows. It will make its way round the baffles to reach the light.

These experiments show that growing plants need warmth and light.

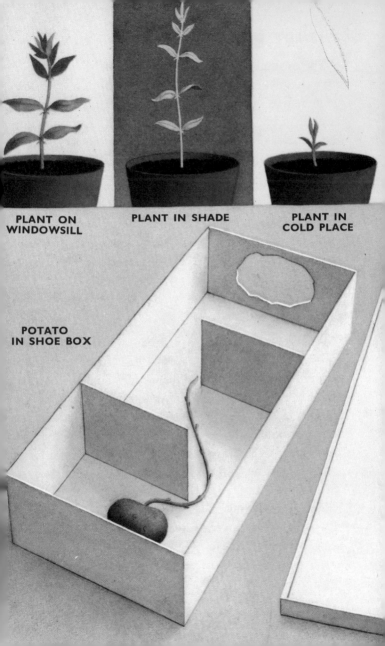

PLANT ON WINDOWSILL

PLANT IN SHADE

PLANT IN COLD PLACE

POTATO IN SHOE BOX

THE LIFE OF A PLANT

The normal life of plants differs widely. A Poppy, for example, is sown, grows and dies all in one season while a tree may live for centuries. Plants which live and die in one season are called *annuals*. Examples are the Scarlet Pimpernel, many garden flowers, Peas, Beans and other vegetables.

Plants which live for two years are called *biennials*, meaning *two years*. They grow up in the first year and form their leaves and then lie dormant all the winter, storing food. In the second year they flower, and feed the flower on the food they have stored. The flower forms the fruit and seed and then the plant dies. The Teasel in the picture is a biennial; you can see it in its first and second year.

Plants which live for a number of years are called *perennials*. They grow every year from spring to autumn and lie dormant in the winter. Some perennials shed their leaves in the autumn and grow new ones in the spring. Other perennials keep their leaves throughout the winter. These two types are explained on the next page. There are also perennials which die back above the ground, but keep a short thick stem underground, called the *rootstock*. This remains alive at the top of the root and grows again in the spring. Rhubarb does this. Nothing can live for ever, of course, and some perennials live for a few years only while big trees can live for hundreds of years.

RHUBARB
PERENNIAL

TEASEL
FIRST YEAR

TEASEL
SECOND YEAR
BIENNIAL

PPY
NUAL

DECIDUOUS BUSHES AND TREES

The perennial plants which shed their leaves in the autumn and lie dormant in the winter, and then grow new leaves in the spring, are called *deciduous*, which is derived from a Latin word meaning 'to fall'.

It is one of the best known sights in nature; the bare trees and hedges turning green in the spring, coming into full leaf for the summer, changing to yellow and gold as the leaves dry and die in the autumn, and being blown about by the wind until they come off to leave bare branches for the winter. But if you look closely you will see that the bare twigs already have their buds, waiting to burst into new leaves in the spring. This we found when we examined twigs on page 10.

In winter you can see the clear shape of a tree, and different trees have different shapes. Think, too, of the size and strength of the roots of a large tree, and how firmly they hold it against the strong winds and gales of winter.

Every spring the bare branches of bushes and trees come to life, as nourishment is taken from the soil by the roots; we say the sap is rising. As the leaves grow so the tree grows. If you examine a sawn-off tree trunk you will notice a number of rings. Each of these represents one year of growth, so by counting them you can tell the age of a tree.

EVERGREENS

All bushes and trees are not deciduous, shedding their leaves in the autumn and growing them again in the spring. Some are *evergreen*, a word which describes itself. The green Holly with its gay red berries, and which we put in our homes at Christmas, is an evergreen. Even in mid-winter the Holly still has all its green leaves.

If you examine a Holly leaf you will see that it is tough and leathery, and much sturdier than the delicate leaf of a deciduous tree.

There are many evergreens, such as the Ivy, the Laurel, which you often see in gardens and parks, and the Bay tree, which provides the leaves that were used in ancient days to crown conquerors and poets. The Yew is an evergreen, too, and was the tree which provided the wood for the bows of the English archers. The Box is another evergreen, and is often used for hedges.

The Fir and Pine trees are all evergreen, but not the Larch. They are called *coniferous*, because they produce their seeds in cones. We have all seen pine cones.

Evergreens produce new leaves on new twigs each spring, but the old leaves remain until they fall off when they are worn out. When you go for a walk in winter notice the different trees, dividing them into the two kinds, the deciduous which are bare, and the evergreens, which still have their leaves.

SPRUCE
CONES

SCOTS
PINE

YEW TREE

HOLLY

CLIMBING PLANTS

Many kinds of plants grow very long stems specially adapted for climbing up other plants to reach the light.

The Blackberry, or Bramble, and the Wild Rose climb by using their sharp thorns to hook on to twigs. The Pea and the Vetch grow small tendrils to grasp twigs to pull themselves up. If you look at a row of Peas in the garden you will see how the tendrils wind themselves tightly round the pea-sticks the gardener puts for them.

The Wild Clematis, also known as 'Old Man's Beard' because the white fluffy fruits look like a white beard, uses another method. It uses the stalks of some of its leaves as tendrils to climb high trees. Honeysuckle, Runner Beans, Convolvulus and Hops wind their stems round the stems of other plants. Look at Beans wound round bean-poles in the garden. The stem of each kind of plant always winds itself in the same direction.

Goosegrass, or Cleavers, has tiny hooks all over the stem and leaves with which it can cling to other plants. Virginia Creeper climbs by using little bunches of suckers to hold on to a wall. Ivy, which we often see growing up the trunks of old trees, anchors itself by putting out small roots from its stem. The Ivy grows two kinds of leaf, five-pointed ones where it is climbing and oval ones at the top, where the flowers grow.

RUNNER BEAN

IVY

BRAMBLE

VETCH

PRICKLES, THORNS AND STINGS

Some plants protect themselves by growing prickles or thorns, or by stinging. Animals avoid eating prickly plants unless the grazing is very poor, and Thistles are usually left standing in a field grazed by cattle. There are exceptions; donkeys can eat Thistles because they have a specially tough tongue, and animals such as camels and goats, which normally live where vegetation is sparse and rough, can eat prickly plants.

The thorns which grow on some plants, such as Roses, are very sharp and curve downwards, and they will scratch an animal's tongue, or your hand when you pick them. You notice the thorns when you pick blackberries.

Everyone who has walked through Nettles with bare legs knows how they sting. The leaves and stems of Nettles are covered with tiny hairs, each sharply pointed and containing a speck of poison. When the pointed hairs stick in your skin the ends break off and the poison makes your skin itch and burn. Fortunately the pain soon passes.

Some plants contain poison which can make cattle ill, or even kill them. The leaves of the Yew tree are poisonous for cattle and horses, and so are the berries to humans. Other poisonous plants are Henbane, Deadly Nightshade—also called Belladonna—and Hemlock. A farmer makes sure none of these plants are growing in his hedges before he puts animals into a field.

The pictures show some of the poisonous plants. They are dangerous, so if you see any—leave them alone.

STINGING NETTLE

HEMLOCK
(POISONOUS)

NBANE
(SONOUS)

DEADLY
NIGHTSHADE
(POISONOUS)

THORNS
OF ROSE

GRASS AND GRAIN

The grasses are a very important group of plants. Grain, which is the fruit of grass, provides the main food for most of the world's human population. These *cereals*, which means grain we can eat, are wheat, oats, barley, rye, maize and rice, and they are all grasses.

Thousands of years ago Early Man made a very important discovery. He found that by cultivating certain kinds of grass he could grow a lot of good quality grain, which he could grind into flour to make bread or porridge, and which he could feed to his cattle in winter.

Most grass is perennial, although one very common kind, Annual Meadow grass, which grows in thick tufts and has feathery heads of flowers, is an annual.

Grass flowers are different from most plants because they do not have petals, but they are very dainty and worth close examination. Grass leaves, the blades of grass, are always long and narrow. Bamboo is a grass and in the tropics it can grow to a height of one hundred and twenty feet, with the stems as thick as tree trunks.

If you dig up a tuft of grass and examine it closely you will see that it is a complete plant, with roots, stem, leaves and, in summertime, the delicate flower with its seeds.

Britain is famous for its rich green fields and fine lawns, for our climate is especially good for growing grass. If you make a collection of grasses you will be surprised to find how many there are.

BAMBOO

WHEAT

OATS

MEADOW
GRASSES

FERNS AND MOSSES

Ferns are plants which seem to break the usual rules; they have neither leaves nor flowers. You might think that the tall delicate Ferns are leaves, but they are not. They are *fronds*, which take the place of both leaves and fruit. If you examine the back of a fern frond you will see neat rows of small brown spots. These contain the *spores* which, when they are free, can develop into new Ferns. Spores are not seeds, though they perform the same function. There are many kinds of Ferns, but they all have the same characteristics: fronds with, on the back, containers of the spores.

The Fern is one of the oldest of plants, its imprint is found in coal, an imprint which may have been made a million years ago or more.

Moss is another plant which does not have true leaves and flowers. It grows in tight green 'cushions', which are composed of hundreds of tiny plants packed close together. You can find Moss on walls, in ledges and gutters, and on stones.

If you examine a cushion of Moss you will notice that the tiny stems have knobs on top. These knobs contain the spores. On a dry day the top of these 'boxes' will come off and the spores will be blown away by the wind. Those which find a resting place where they can grow will become new plants.

Ferns and Mosses are an interesting study and, as with most plants, there are many different kinds. This is another interesting subject for the collector.

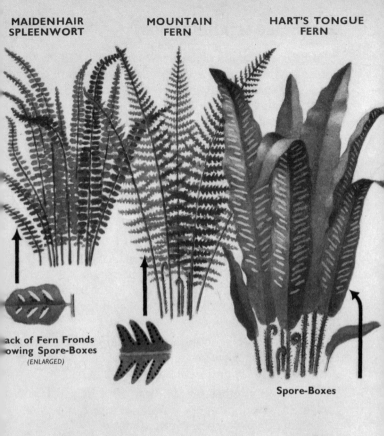

MAIDENHAIR SPLEENWORT

MOUNTAIN FERN

HART'S TONGUE FERN

ack of Fern Fronds
owing Spore-Boxes
(ENLARGED)

Spore-Boxes

FRAGMENTS OF THREE DIFFERENT KINDS OF MOSSES *(ENLARGED)*

FUNGI, ALGAE AND LICHEN

Fungi is the name given to Mushrooms and Toad-stools; a Mushroom is a *fungus*. Mushrooms are good to eat, but many Toadstools are poisonous and should be left strictly alone.

Fungi do not have proper roots, they depend on other plants for their food and grow where another kind of plant has rotted away. The Mushroom we pick is only the part of the plant which carries the spores, the real plant is the little white hairs underground, which look like roots. Fungi are not green because they do not contain chlorophyll.

At first the Mushroom consists of a round knob, contained in an 'envelope' on a stem. As it grows the 'envelope' is broken, leaving a ring round the stem. The knob becomes the curved cap of the ripe Mushroom, with gills underneath, from which the spores fall to make new Mushrooms.

The Puff-ball is a simple form of fungus, consisting of a bag of spores which burst open when ripe. Fungi grow very quickly and have a very short life.

The *alga* is another simple form of plant which you find as a green powdery substance on damp walls. Some pond plants and seaweed are algae.

Lichen grows in damp places and you find it on old walls and trees. It is similar to Moss, but it is actually two plants living together, one a fungus and the other an alga. The fungus gets a grip on the wall, stone or tree and the alga then joins it. The fungus holds on, which the alga cannot do, and the alga provides the food for both. The fungus makes spores in little cup-shaped containers, or some in containers like trumpets.

SHINING
POLYPORUS

LICHEN ON TREE TRUNK

'UFF BALL

TOADSTOOLS

LICHEN
ON TWIG

AMANITA
MUSCARIA
(POISONOUS)

MUSHROOMS

WATER PLANTS

Certain kinds of plants are specially adapted to grow in or near water. Some float on the water, like the Frog-bit and Duckweed we see on ponds, and other plants live under the water.

The Water Crowfoot lives partly under water and partly out of it, and it has two kinds of leaf, the hair-like leaves under water and the leaves like Clover or Shamrock above the surface. It has pretty white flowers in spring, shaped like Buttercups. Another plant, the Water Soldier, floats below the surface, but rises in July to flower.

Water-lilies are one of the loveliest flowers in Britain, and both the white and the smaller yellow flowers are quite common. The white Water-lily flower rises above the surface of the water each day to open in the sunlight, and the petals close at night as it sinks below the surface. It has round plate-like leaves which float on the surface.

The beautiful Flowering Rush, the Yellow Iris, and the giant Reed Mace, the flower we call the Bulrush, grow on the banks of ponds and streams.

Meadowsweet and Kingcups are found on pond and river banks, in wet meadows and sometimes in ditches. There are many kinds of reeds which flourish in meres, lakes and marshes. The world of fish and water fowl has a wealth of lovely plants.

PARASITES AND THE SUNDEW

Parasites are plants which live on others. Mistletoe grows on certain trees. If a Mistletoe berry falls into the ground it will not grow, but it frequently grows, and flourishes, on the branch of an Apple tree.

The Broom-rape is a parasite which grows on the roots of Broom or Furze bushes. It is not pretty, but it is an interesting plant to find. The Toothwort is rather similar and sometimes you can find it in woods and thickets growing on the roots of Hazel.

The Dodder, which grows on Gorse, Heather and Thyme is a strange and pretty plant with long thread-like stems and bunches of pink waxy flowers, like beads on a string. It never has leaves. The seeds of the Dodder germinate on the ground under the bush it will use, the young stems climb up and attach themselves to the bush and when they are established the stems break and all connexion with the ground is broken.

The Sundew is not a parasite, but it has the strange habit of living on flies. The plant is found in bogs and marshes. The leaves, like small plates, are covered with sticky red hairs. When an unfortunate fly settles on them it is caught by the hairs which then curl over, trapping the victim. When the plant has absorbed the juice of the fly it opens again to await the next victim. Not a nice plant, but very interesting.

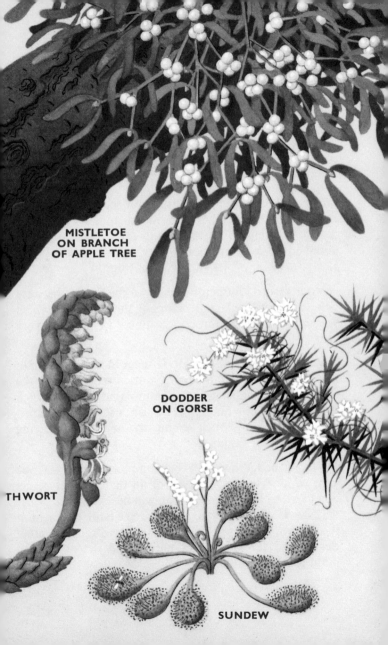

MISTLETOE
ON BRANCH
OF APPLE TREE

DODDER
ON GORSE

THWORT

SUNDEW

BOTANY AS A HOBBY

There is no end to the delight in finding out about plants, from the smallest wild flower to the greatest tree, and getting to know their species and their ways. The botanist, the name for the student of plants, knows how to observe and how to recognise what he sees. With a good reference book and advice from an expert, you can become an amateur botanist.

It is a good plan to keep a notebook, in which you can record anything interesting you see. Put the date and place, the weather conditions and, if your discovery is likely to be something rare, have the entry initialled by a companion who was with you. *Do not pick really rare plants*—leave them to grow.

Your record will be of interest in the future, because you can look back and compare the dates on which you saw the first Primrose, say, or wild Daffodil, every year.

You can collect leaves, press them in newspaper in a heavy book and fix them in your notebook with the name, and perhaps with the Latin name as well, which shows the plant's family. You can also collect plants, and special kinds such as mosses and ferns, sorting them into their families.

Find a hedgerow on a bank and examine just one yard of it. Then make a list of all the different plants you can find in that yard. You will be astonished at the variety. If you study that same yard of bank throughout the season, from spring to winter, you will learn a great deal about the wonder of nature and the miracle of plant life and growth.

INDEX

EFFECT OF LIGHT ON LEAVES AND STEMS

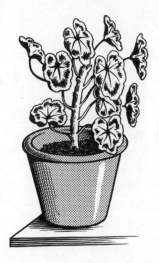

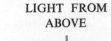
LIGHT FROM ONE SIDE

LIGHT FROM ABOVE

LIGHT FROM ABOVE AND SIDES

DRAWINGS SHOW HOW LEAVES WILL TAKE UP A POSITION APPROXIMATELY AT RIGHT ANGLES TO THE DIRECTION OF LIGHT

Series 651

This is a book that will interest readers of all ages, as there is endless delight in finding out about plant-life.

With clear text and full-colour illustrations it will help to give a greater understanding of plants, their basic features and how they grow, feed, protect and reproduce themselves. It also describes some easy but fascinating experiments for which only the simplest of materials are required.